The MacMagics

A Spell For My Sister

Barron's Arch Book Series

The MacMagics

A Spell For My Sister

Terrance Dicks

Illustrated by Celia Canning

First edition for the United States and the Philippines published 1992 by Barron's Educational Series, Inc.

First published 1991 by Piccadilly Press Ltd., London, England

All inquiries should be addressed to:
Barron's Educational Series, Inc.
250 Wireless Boulevard
Hauppauge, New York 11788

International Standard Book No. 0-8120-4881-4

Library of Congress Catalog Card No. 91-32661

Library of Congress Cataloging-in-Publication Data

Dicks, Terrace.
A spell for my sister / Terrance Dicks; illustrated by Celia Canning.—1st ed. for the U.S. and the Philippines.
p. cm.—(Barron's arch book series) (The MacMagics) "First published 1991 by Piccadilly Press Ltd., London, England"—T.p. verso.
Summary: Mike MacMagic, the youngest in a family of witches, wizards, and magicians, suspects his sister's new boyfriend of foul play when family heirlooms start to disapperar and his sister's behavior changes.
ISBN 0-8120-4881-4
[1. Magic—Fiction. 2. Witches—Fiction.] I. Canning, Celia, ill. II.. Title. III. Series. IV. Series: Dicks, Terrance. MacMagics.
PZ7.D5627Sp 1992
[Fic]—dc20

91-32661
CIP
AC

PRINTED IN THE UNITED STATES OF AMERICA
2345 9770 987654321

CONTENTS

About the Author

After studying at Cambridge, Terrance Dicks became an advertising copywriter, then a radio and television scriptwriter and script editor. His career as an author began with the *Dr. Who* series and he has now written a variety of other books on subjects ranging from horror to detection. Barron's publishes several of his series, including *The Adventures of Goliath, T.R. Bear, A Cat Called Max,* and *The MacMagics.*

Chapter One

The Missing Slipper Mystery

"Slippers!" yelled Dad.

A single slipper came hopping down the stairs.

It landed at Dad's feet, quivering with eagerness like a well-trained spaniel.

"I said slippers! Two feet, two slippers! *Other slipper*! "

You can always tell when Dad's upset—he screams all over the place. The first slipper quivered, but no second slipper came down to join it.

Mom was mixing messy-looking herbal potions at the kitchen table. "Maybe the summoning spell's faded, dear."

Dad scowled at her. "My spells never fade!"

"Just as well if it has," Mom went on, ignoring him as usual. "You're the one who's always saying we shouldn't use magic for trivial domestic purposes. You should go and get your slippers like anyone else. The exercise would do you good."

If there's one thing Dad hates, it's being criticized, especially when he's wrong. Ignoring Mom, he looked around the room—and saw me. "Just run upstairs and find my other slipper, would you, Mike old boy?"

"Sorry, Dad," I said regretfully. "Homework! You wouldn't want to ruin my education, would you?"

Gran appeared, her cat Grimalkin on her shoulder. At the sight of Grimalkin, the single slipper twitched nervously. With a yowl, Grimalkin leaped from Gran's shoulder and pounced on it, shaking it like a rat.

"So that's what happened to my other

slipper," snarled Dad. "That mangy beast of yours has probably eaten it!"

He snatched the slipper back—or rather, he tried to. But Grimalkin's a big, tough, mean old cat, and he refused to let go.

"Leave my Grimalkin alone," screeched Gran. "Let him play with it if he wants it. One slipper's no use to you anyway!"

"That is just the point," thundered Dad. "I used to have two! I'll skin the creature and have a nice pair in catskin instead!"

"You'll do no such thing, you evil brute.

You always were a nasty little boy!"

At this point Grandpa arrived and joined in. He grabbed Grimalkin and tried to pull him away from the slipper.

Letting go of the slipper, Grimalkin bit him.

With a yell of rage, Grandpa ran after Grimalkin who sneered and dodged and streaked up to the top of the curtains. Gran squawked and turned her attention to Grandpa. She snapped her fingers and shot a quick magical thunderbolt at him.

Grandpa threw up a magic shield and shot back a fireball in return.

Gran ducked and the fireball sizzled over her head, shattering a flower vase.

Grandpa and Gran faced each other, and Dad rose to his feet.

"Stop that! Or do you want a quick trip to the North and South Poles, respectively?"

He could do it too, and they both knew it.

Gran and Grandpa subsided, muttering.

"Really!" said Mom. "You're like children, all of you!"

I was just about to object to this blatantly anti-child remark when my brother Murdo staggered in, huddled in his black cloak and rubbing his red eyes.

"Do you all have to make so much noise? You woke me up and it's not even dark yet. Look, who stole my cloak?"

"You're wearing it!" I said.

"Not this one—my old one. This is my new one; I was saving it for a special occasion."

"Saving it to haunt the higher class churchyards, I suppose?" Murdo's a vampire.

Well, he's not really a vampire—he's an art student, though you never seem to see him study. He's also a squeamish wimp who faints at the sight of blood. In spite of this, he's in love with the vampire life-style—or do I mean death-style? Anyway, you know what I mean. Black cloaks, coffins, graveyards, the whole bit, and he never gets up before evening if he can avoid it.

He was followed by my sister Meg, who was also looking a bit annoyed. "Do we have to have all this racket?"

Just one big happy family, as you can see.

Maybe it's time I introduced us.

We're the MacMagics.

The imposing-looking gentleman in the fuzzy plaid socks is Dad, Professor Malcolm MacMagic.

The eccentrically-dressed lady is Mom, Doctor Martha MacMagic, New-Age

therapist, healer and good witch.

The whiskery old gentleman is Grandpa Mortimer MacMagic, once known at Mysterious Mortimer, retired stage magician and practicing wizard—and believe me, practice is just what he needs.

And the grumpy-looking old lady with the pointed hat is Granny Maggie MacMagic. Gran's a traditional old-fashioned witch—pointed hat, nose and chin, with a flying broomstick and a black cat, Grimalkin, whom you've already met.

You already know the guy in the black cloak, my brother Murdo, the would-be vampire.

The pretty girl with the short hair and the big glasses is Meg MacMagic, my sister. She's a witch too, of course, the young and pretty kind.

Meg has a special power called the Glamor. Unless she's very careful, every man she meets falls madly in love with her. This might seem like a good thing, but it can happen whether Meg wants it to or not, and it's no joke fending off some creep you can't stand.

She tries to play down the effect of the Glamor by making herself look plain.

Then there's me, Mike MacMagic, just a normal healthy school kid. At least I'd like to be, but with a family like mine it isn't easy.

I mean, you may think your family's weird, but just look at mine. Two wizards, three witches, and one wannabe vampire!

"What is all the fuss about?" asked Meg impatiently.

Mom sniffed. "Your father's lost one of his slippers."

"Is that all?" said Meg grumpily. "I thought it was a real catastrophe."

"It is a catastrophe," said Dad sulkily. "I loved those slippers."

"It's time you got rid of those awful old things anyway," said Meg, and threw herself into a chair.

I looked at her in mild surprise. Usually Meg was the nicest of the family, the one least likely to throw a fit. Maybe all the waiting was getting on her nerves. She was an actress when she got the chance, but like most actresses, she spent a lot of time at home, just waiting for the phone to ring.

Mom got up. "It's time I was thinking about dinner. Has anyone seen my cookbook?

I couldn't find it earlier."

"Which one?" asked Meg. "You've got dozens of them."

"It's an old favorite, Traditional Scottish Recipes. I thought I'd have another try at making a haggis."

I shuddered. Haggis is a kind of meat and oatmeal pudding—not exactly one of my favorites. "Don't, Mom, please," I begged. "Remember last time!"

Mom's cooking's a bit erratic, and she tends to use magical shortcuts. She'd decided her last haggis was a bit dull so she magicked so much life into it that it grew legs and dashed off down the street!

Dad was opening a letter that had arrived in the afternoon mail. "It's from the IPM!" he said. "They've asked me to be President. I'm to take office at the next Annual General Meeting."

"That's nice, dear," said Mom. "Will you accept?"

"Oh, I suppose I shall have to," said Dad. "Kind of a bore really..."

But you could see he was really flattered.

The IPM, the Institute of Practitioners in Magic, is an association of all the top sorcerers. It's an honor to even be a member, let alone President.

Suddenly Dad chuckled. "It's a slap in the face for Auld Mac, isn't it? He'll be chewing his whiskers up there in the misty Highlands of Scotland."

"We must celebrate," said Grandpa. Grandpa's always looking for an excuse to reach for his crab apple juice.

We all drank to Dad's health. "Who's this Auld Mac?" I asked.

"The MacAroon of MacAroon," said Grandpa. "We've had a feud with the Clan MacAroon since time immemorial. They're our deadly rivals. Auld Mac is their chieftain and he's desperate to be President. He'll have a fit when he hears they've chosen your father!"

"Childish nonsense," sniffed Mom. She's never had much patience for the Institute.

The doorbell rang, and Meg jumped a foot in the air. "That'll be for me. Don't bother

about dinner for me, Mom. I'm going out."

Dad decided to play the strict father. "And with whom, may I ask?"

"With a friend of mine. His name's Angus."

Mom raised an eyebrow. "Ask him in for a moment, dear. We'd all like to meet him."

Meg didn't seem too happy about that, and with a family like ours I didn't blame her. But when Mom uses her special steel-fist-in-a-velvet-glove voice it's no use arguing.

The doorbell rang again and Meg went to answer it.

She returned a few minutes later with a strange young man. He was tall, dark and handsome in a bony sort of way, dressed up in a stylish suit. "This is Angus, everyone," she said rapidly. "Angus, meet Mom and Dad, Gran and Grandpa, and my two brothers, Murdo and Mike."

There was a general mumbling of "hellos," and "pleased-to-meet-yous." Then Meg said brightly, "Well, we must be off!"

"You'll have a wee drink before you go, young fellow," said Grandpa, reaching for the decanter of crab apple juice.

"Well, just a small one," said Angus. His voice had a very faint Scots accent, and he looked almost as uncomfortable as Meg.

Grandpa poured a small glass of juice for Angus and another large one for himself. "And what brings you to our little town?"

Before Angus could answer Meg said, "Angus has opened a shop—in the new shopping mall."

"What kind of a shop?" asked Mom.

"A magic shop," said Angus. Eyebrows shot up all around.

Angus said, "Not real magic. We sell electronic toys and games, magic tricks,

computer games, Dungeons and Dragons. The shop's called AM Games."

"I must come and have a look," said Grandpa. "I know a few magic tricks myself. I used to be on the stage, you know. Perhaps you've heard of me? Mysterious Mortimer!"

"Come along, Angus," said Meg firmly. "We really must be going!" She grabbed Angus's hand and dragged him out of the room.

I couldn't help feeling a bit puzzled.

Young Angus seemed to be pretty much the ideal boyfriend, the kind who gets along well with the whole family. So, why had Meg

been so reluctant to introduce him, so eager to get away?

Maybe the romance wasn't going so well. It was none of my business really, but I couldn't help worrying all the same. I'd always been extra-fond of Meg. We'd gotten along well ever since we were little. We used to have long talks about things the rest of the family just didn't understand. I was the first one she told about her dream of being an actress, and I remember telling her about my strange ambition to be an ordinary kid in an ordinary school.

We hadn't had one of our talks for quite some time.

It wasn't just Meg, though. I had an uneasy feeling that something strange was going to happen—and I was right!

Tomorrow was going to be the strangest, most dangerous day the MacMagics had ever had to face.

It started when I discovered my teddy bear was missing...

Chapter Two

Mayhem in the Mall

All right, so I'm too old for a teddy bear.

But I'd had Old Ted ever since I was tiny. His fur was wearing thin by now and he was missing one ear and one eye, but I was still very fond of him. I didn't take him to bed anymore of course, but I kept him on a shelf with some other outgrown odds and ends like model airplanes and my Action Man.

I didn't notice he was missing when I went to bed, but I spotted it as soon as I woke up.

Usually the first thing I saw was Old Ted's beady eye twinkling at me from his place on the shelf. But now he was gone.

Feeling like a fool, I asked the family about it over breakfast. It was Saturday morning and they all straggled down one by one—all except Murdo, of course.

Everyone denied any knowledge of the missing Ted.

"You didn't take it for one of your charity bazaars?" I asked Mom suspiciously.

"Of course not, dear. I wouldn't take it without asking you, and besides, who'd buy the poor old thing?"

I sometimes think Mom would sell *me* for a charity bazaar if she could, but that last argument convinced me. Old Ted simply had no market value. So, who'd want to steal him? And why?

"Where's Meg?" I asked.

"She's had her breakfast already. I think she said she was going shopping," said Mom vaguely.

"Maybe she'll buy you a new teddy bear," cackled Gran, feeding Grimalkin a bit of bacon.

I gulped down my juice and toast. "I'll see if I can catch her before she goes..."

Leaving Dad muttering about "Uncivilized behavior at the breakfast-table..." I shot out of the room—just in time to hear the front door close.

I thought about trying to talk to Murdo but realized he'd be fast asleep, so I decided to go after Meg. By the time I got out of the house, she was at the far end of the street.

"Meg!" I called. "Hold on a minute..." She didn't hear and I set off after her.

She was trotting along very quickly, and before I could catch up she led me to a massive glass building dominating the center of town—our new shopping mall.

It was pretty much like any other shopping mall—a huge glass hall lined with two different levels of shops, escalators and fountains at one end and enough potted palms to make a Tarzan movie jungle.

The place was already crowded with Saturday morning shoppers, and at first I couldn't see her anywhere. Then I spotted her going into a store near one of the fountains. It was a place called AM Games.

Suddenly everything became clear, especially when Angus appeared in the doorway to meet her and clasped her in his arms. I sat down on the little wall surrounding the pool, wondering what to do next.

I couldn't very well speak to Meg now. She'd only think I'd been spying on her. I was just about to leave when I noticed something strange.

There was magic in the air, hanging like a faint, scarcely visible mist.

I looked curiously around the mall. It was like a fake studio jungle, I thought, though in a movie there'd be a monster lurking in the pool.

I glanced down at the water and saw the strange mist floating on the surface. Beneath it the water started to bubble and seethe. A long rubbery arm with feelers on it snaked out of the pool and pulled me inside.

I splashed into the pool with a yell of alarm and began frantically thrashing around trying to escape from my attacker.

When I got out—if I got out—I'd complain to the management, I thought. Palms and fountains were all very nice, but a giant octopus was carrying things too far.

I was yelling and shouting so much that a large crowd gathered and someone leaned over the pool, grabbed me by the collar and hauled me out.

I looked up spluttering, and found myself facing a big, bushy-mustached character in a security guard's uniform.

"Can't you read, sonny?" He pointed to a notice. "STRICTLY NO SWIMMING."

"I wasn't swimming!"

"And what were you doing, may I ask?"

I turned and pointed indignantly into the pool. "I was—" I was just about to say, "pulled into the pool by a great big octopus!"

Then I saw that the pool was actually quite small and, apart from a few floating drink cartons, quite empty. The strange mist had gone, you could see right to the bottom—and there was no sign of a giant octopus anywhere.

"I was leaning back and I fell over," I finished weakly. "Sorry!"

The guard sighed wearily and turned away, and I trudged off to the men's room to dry out. Once I was alone, a quick dehydration spell took care of the sogginess, and I came back out into the mall, determined to find out what was going on.

One thing was clear—I had been the victim of a magic attack, a magical illusion so powerful that I'd thought it was real.

I remembered the magical mist I'd noticed earlier.

I decided to wait for Meg after all, and see what she thought about things.

It was a bad decision...

I got bored sitting still and started

wandering up and down, keeping an eye on the door of the games shop in case Meg came out.

I was walking past a particularly thick clump of potted palms, thinking again how much the place looked like a studio jungle. It looked like the sort of place where you'd expect to find Tarzan, wrestling with a gorilla.

Suddenly I noticed a faint mist floating all around.

A massive hairy hand on the end of a long hairy arm reached out and grabbed me by the shoulder, hauling me into the bushes. Wrenching myself free, I jumped back and looked up at my attacker.

It was a giant gorilla, a regular King Kong.

For a moment we glared at each other. Then the gorilla roared and pounded its chest. Apparently they do that to frighten their enemies, and it was certainly working on me!

Then I remembered I was a MacMagic.

I stared hard at the gorilla, telling myself it was just an illusion, just an illusion…It worked too!

The gorilla looked disappointed and started to become transparent.

It was almost on the point of fading away when some unseen enemy fought back with a sudden surge of magical energy.

The gorilla become solid again, and it grew even larger!

Towering over the potted palms it pounded its chest and gave a shattering roar.

A lady going by with her shopping bags looked up and gave an ear-piercing shriek. Alarmed by the scream, the other shoppers looked up and saw a giant gorilla howling and gnashing his teeth amid the potted palms.

Moms and dads and kids, grannies and grandads all turned and stampeded for the exits.

I was halfway to the nearest exit myself when I heard a loud scream in a familiar voice. "Mike! Mike!"

I turned and saw that, just as in the movie, the giant gorilla had snatched up a pretty girl. He was holding her up before his face and peering curiously at her, as she struggled wildly in the grip of the giant hand.

The pretty girl he'd grabbed was my sister Meg!

Chapter Three

Disappearing Trick

Suddenly everything froze—and blurred and disappeared. I heard a voice call, "Mike! Mike, are you all right?"

I blinked hard, and then opened my eyes.

Meg was standing in front of me, Angus beside her. They both looked very worried.

I looked around. No octopus, no giant gorilla, no screaming crowd fleeing for the exits.

Things weren't quite back to normal though. People were milling around and chattering excitedly.

"I tell you I saw it," some man was saying. "A great big hairy ape! It had grabbed this girl..."

"Come on!" said his wife. "You were probably asleep on your feet and having a nightmare. Now, let's go, we've still got a week's food shopping to do."

Similar conversations were going on all around us. Some people had seen something; some people hadn't.

Lots of people thought something strange had happened, but they weren't sure what.

The whole crowd seemed to be nervous and excited, and several arguments broke out. I even saw the big security man breaking up a fight.

Meg and Angus seemed to be just as confused as everyone else.

"I came to do some shopping and stopped in to see Angus," said Meg. "When I came out of his shop everyone was shouting and milling around. Then I saw you standing there in a sort of trance..."

Angus didn't have much to add. "I heard some kind of fuss going on outside when Meg left the shop, and came out to make sure she was all right. I pushed my way through the crowd and found both of you right here..."

The fuss was dying down now and people were getting back to their shopping.

Angus was looking at me with concern. "You look pretty shaken. Would you like to

sit down and have something to drink?"

There was a circular area at the other end of the mall, filled with wooden chairs and tables and surrounded by different kinds of food stalls. Meg and I sat down and Angus brought two cups of coffee for him and Meg and a milkshake and a hamburger for me. Somehow all the excitement had left me feeling hungry.

As I was starting to eat, Angus said awkwardly, "You were out in the mall all the time. What do you think happened?"

I caught an anxious look from Meg, and

guessed that she didn't want any talk about magic in front of Angus.

I swallowed a bit of hamburger and shrugged. "Hard to say. All the noise and the crowds seemed to make my head swim. I felt dizzy and heard a lot of shouting..."

"It was probably a sort of mass hysteria," said Meg. "Something to do with the lighting and the design of the mall."

"I hope they get it fixed soon," said Angus gloomily. "It'll no' be very good for business! Speaking of which, I'd better go and reopen my shop."

I wandered tactfully off to let Meg and Angus say their goodbyes. It seemed to take them quite a while, and I looked back and saw them in agitated conversation. The whole business seemed to have upset them both quite a bit.

Meg gave Angus a quick kiss and hurried to join me.

She seemed silent and worried on the way home, and once again I had the feeling there was something wrong.

"What do you think all that was about?" I said at last.

Meg shot me an angry glance. "You ought to know!"

I was astonished—and hurt at the same time. "Me?"

"Yes, you! You were the one causing that ape illusion—and let me tell you, I didn't enjoy it a bit! It's a good thing you stopped it in time!"

"You've got it all wrong," I said indignantly. "I admit I was thinking about gorillas, but I didn't cause the illusion, and I didn't stop it either. Something plucked the idea out of my mind and lifted it...

Something's going on, Meg. I'm going to tell Dad about it when I get home."

"I wouldn't do that if I were you. You know how Dad hates any kind of public fuss. If he even thinks you had anything to do with what happened, you'll be in trouble!"

"Maybe you're right. Though he's bound to find out..."

I'd seen some of our neighbors in that mall, and they'd been looking at me suspiciously.

"Well, suit yourself," snapped Meg.

I gave her a puzzled look. "Is something the matter, Meg?"

"How do you mean?"

"We never used to fight like this."

Meg frowned for a moment, then had a sudden change of mood. She grinned at me, and all at once she was the old Meg again. "Don't be so silly, Mike. Everything's all right." She ruffled my hair. "Your trouble is, you just don't understand women!"

"Who does?" I grumbled. "I don't think you understand yourselves!"

All the same I felt better—for a while.

When we got home, I put my key in the lock to open the front door.

There was a flash of light, an explosion that knocked us both head-over-heels, and a cloud of green smoke from which there appeared a tall and terrifying figure.

It was Grandpa, all dressed up in his wizard's cloak and pointed hat.

He cackled evilly. "That'll teach you, you wicked old woman—oh, dear, I am sorry!"

The smoke had cleared and he could see me and Meg picking ourselves up from the front path.

It had been a hard morning, and I was beginning to feel I'd had enough. "Just what do you think you're doing? I've a good mind to send you off to the Sahara for a while!"

I've got a fair amount of the Power myself when I choose to use it, and Grandpa knew this was no idle threat. He backed away, raising his hands. "No need to take it like that, Michael, my boy! It was only a bit of firework magic—no real harm done. It wasn't intended for you anyway."

Meg brushed herself off. "Who was it meant for?"

"Gran, of course," I said. I looked sternly at Grandpa. "What's she done to upset you this time?"

"She's stolen my smoking jacket!"

Grandpa's smoking jacket was his pride and joy. It was an elaborate Edwardian affair in red velvet, covered with ornamental embroidery and trimmed with gold braid. It had been a present from the great Houdini and Grandpa liked to wear it as he sat working on his memoirs of life on the stage.

"How do you know it was Gran who took your smoking jacket?"

"Well, it's missing, isn't it? And who else would play such a stupid trick?"

He had a point. The long-running feud between Gran and Grandpa was a permanent feature of life in the MacMagic household.

Stealing the old man's smoking jacket was just the sort of silly thing Gran would do—provoked, very probably, by some equally dumb trick from Grandpa himself.

Suddenly I noticed something strange—a faint mist hanging in the air in our front garden...

With a piercing shriek a huge black shape swooped down from the rooftop, knocked Grandpa flying, and shot back up into the sky.

I looked up and saw Gran on her broomstick, circling around for another dive.

She was brandishing her big old umbrella. "Steal my Grimalkin, would you? Well, you can just bring him right back or I'll batter you black and blue!"

To prove she meant it, she dived down again and gave Grandpa a swipe with the umbrella that made him howl with rage.

"Never mind that mangy feline!" he shrieked. "Where's my smoking jacket, you horrible old hag?"

He snapped his fingers and shot up a magical thunderbolt that nearly blasted Gran from her broomstick.

She swerved neatly aside, looped the loop, and then dive-bombed Grandpa again, catching him with another crack from the umbrella. He howled and took to his heels, heading for the cover of the little clump of trees close to the house, with Gran after him.

"We won't get any sense out of those two for a while," I said. "Not till they calm down anyway. Let's go inside."

"Shouldn't we try to stop them?"

I shrugged. "I doubt if we could. Anyway, you know they never do any real damage."

That was my second bad decision.

We found Mom in the kitchen looking frantic.

"I'm having a terrible morning," she announced. "Gran and Grandpa have started fighting again..."

Meg said, "I know. We've just seen them."

"We've had a pretty weird morning ourselves," I said. "Something very strange happened in the mall." I told her all about it.

Mom looked worried. "I don't like the sound of it, Michael. There are bad vibrations around today—I've got a sense of something evil going on. I tried to talk to your father about it, but as usual he doesn't want to know."

Dad spends most of his time in his study working on his *History of Magic*. He says scholarship needs absolute peace and quiet and no interruptions, but I think it's just a good excuse for dodging anything difficult.

"Will you talk to him?" said Mom. "You're the only one who can do anything with him."

"If I have to," I said, but I wasn't happy about the idea. Disturbing Dad at work can be a tricky business. I'd had several quick trips to the Sahara already, and I hadn't enjoyed my time as a beetle at all.

"Let me see if I can sort things out myself first," I said.

That made my third bad decision.

I didn't realize just how much trouble we were in...

Chapter Four

Mysterious Meg

The phone rang and Mom answered it. "Yes, this is Doctor MacMagic. Yes, Mrs. Willoughby. What? What? Oh, my goodness! Yes, I'll come over right away."

She slammed down the phone and reached for her cloak.

Mrs. Willoughby was another of Mom's patients, a large fierce lady with a small meek husband.

"What's up with Mrs. Willoughby?" I asked.

"It's not her, it's Mr. Willoughby. Mrs. Willoughby complained he just snored in front of the television all evening, so I gave her an Energizing Potion for him, just to perk him up a little."

"Didn't it work?"

Mom paused at the door. "All too well! The Ladies Flower Arranging Group met at her house this morning, and Mr. Willoughby chased all of them around the garden. They've locked him in the greenhouse and she wants me to come over and calm him down."

"Well, don't overdo it," I said. "Sounds like the most fun he's had in years!"

Mom went off, Meg went to her room, and I started pottering around the kitchen, making myself some hot chocolate and toast for a mid-morning snack. Just as I was finishing it, Dad came thundering down the stairs.

"Where's my morning coffee?"

Dad's the original male chauvinist magician. He breaks for coffee and muffins mid-morning, and expects to find it all ready and waiting for him on a neat little tray.

"Still in the pot," I said. "Mom had to make an emergency house call."

"Couldn't she find time to pour my coffee first?"

"Not without the Ladies Flower Arranging Group risking a fate worse than death," I said "Here, sit down. I'll get you some coffee."

Meg came back into the kitchen, carrying a big shopping bag. "There you are, Dad," she said. "I've got a present for you." Dad

cheered up at once. He loves getting presents.

Meg handed him a handsome pair of fur-lined slippers. "To make up for the one that was lost."

"That's very thoughtful of you, my dear." He sat down and started trying them on.

Meg pulled a glossy-looking book out of the bag. "I got Mom a new cookbook as well. I've even got something for you too, Mike."

She produced a brand new teddy bear. "I know he can't take the place of Old Ted, but still..."

"Thanks anyway," I said. "Pity you couldn't get Grandpa a smoking jacket and Gran a new cat—not that she'd accept any substitute for Grimalkin."

"I'm sure he's just gone on the prowl," said Meg. "He'll turn up."

The phone rang again and Meg answered it. "Hello? Oh, hello Mom... Yes, he's here... It's Mom, Dad. She wants to speak to you."

Dad took the phone and listened, the scowl on his face growing blacker by the minute. Finally he snapped, "Yes, yes, all right, I'll come at once."

He slammed down the phone. "There's

some sort of trouble in town. Your grandparents are mixed up in it, needless to say."

"Do you want me to come and help?" I asked.

"No!" thundered Dad. "Stay here, both of you—and try to stay out of trouble."

A few minutes later we heard him slamming out of the house, leaving me and Meg alone in the kitchen.

Almost immediately Meg started heading for the door.

"Where are you off to?" I asked.

She gave me a startled look. "Oh, here and there. I've got things to do..."

"Don't rush off. Stay and talk to me. Here, have some coffee, I heated some up for Dad."

Before she could refuse I poured a mug of coffee and put it in front of her.

We both sat down at the table. Meg took a sip of coffee, then sat staring into her cup.

We didn't seem to have anything to say to each other.

It felt weird. I was more and more convinced that there was something very mysterious about the way Meg was acting.

"Is everything all right?" I asked.

"Yes, of course. Why shouldn't it be?"

But she still wouldn't look up.

I wondered if it had anything to do with Angus.

Meg had had boyfriends before, though none of them seemed to last very long. I think the real trouble was the Glamor, Meg's magic power. She was so afraid of attracting people for the wrong reasons that she tended to put them off altogether.

"How's Angus?" I asked, and Meg jumped as if I'd jabbed her with a pin.

"Bingo!" I thought. "It is boyfriend trouble."

Meg was looking at me now all right. She was glaring at me. "What do you mean, how's Angus? What about him?"

"Nothing about him, I just asked how he was. When are you seeing him again?"

"He's very busy... He's got a lot of worries, setting up the new shop."

They must have had some sort of argument, I thought, and she didn't want to talk to me about it. I felt a bit hurt to tell the truth, but it was her business, not mine.

"If there's anything I can do..." I said awkwardly.

She looked up and stared hard at me for a long time.

"Mike," she began. "There's something I..."

Suddenly the front door opened and we heard the sound of angry voices.

They belonged to Mom and Dad and Grandma and Grandpa, all arguing furiously.

The family was back!

They poured into the kitchen, all yelling at each other, charges and countercharges echoing around the kitchen.

Suddenly I'd had enough. I jumped to my feet and yelled, "Stop it, all of you!"

An astonished silence fell.

"Now then, would somebody please tell me what's been going on?"

They all opened their mouths to shout again and I said hurriedly, "Just you, please, Father!"

In a quietly furious voice Dad said, "Your grandparents have been staging a dogfight over the center of town. Gran has been

zooming around on her broomstick, while Grandpa pursued her, attempting to bring her down with magical thunderbolts. Apparently he scored a direct hit over the middle of town. By the time I arrived, your grandmother was threatening to turn everyone in sight into a toad, and your grandfather was under arrest for an unauthorized public fireworks display. They were surrounded by a large and angry crowd. I had to use a Time Freeze spell to get us all away in one piece."

No wonder he was so mad. Dad hates using magic in public.

He looked angrily around the room. "You all know how important it is not to attract attention to ourselves. It's actually dangerous —prejudice against those with the Power is very easily aroused." He drew a deep breath. "It is particularly important that we all maintain a low profile at the present time— now that I'm to be President of the Institute of Practitioners in Magic..."

"So that's why he's so worked up, "I thought. "If the MacMagics are involved in a public scandal, the Institute will withdraw the offer."

"I want you all to be particularly careful in the future," Dad went on. "Is that fully understood?"

I looked guiltily at Meg, hoping he didn't get to hear about King Kong in the mall. I didn't dare tell him about it now.

"Tried to murder me, you did!" screeched Gran, looking at Grandpa. "My best broom-stick blown to smithereens!"

"Well, you shouldn't have attacked me, you silly old hag!"

"And you shouldn't have kidnapped Grimalkin."

Suddenly there was a frantic scratching and yowling.

Grimalkin shot through the open window, landing right on Gran's shoulder.

She grabbed him and hugged him till he yowled again.

"Well, that's a relief," said Mom, trying to make peace as usual. "I expect that fuss in town will soon blow over. It's lucky I saw what was happening and called Father. I was just on my way to Mrs. Willoughby when I saw… oh no! Mr. Willoughby—I forgot all about him! I must go over at once."

But it was already too late.

At that very moment we heard screams from the street outside. Mom ran to the front door and we all followed.

Pounding up the street like a herd of elephants in full flight was a group of very large ladies, some of them still clutching bunches of flowers.

Dashing after them like an exceptionally eager sheepdog was a wispy little man with a mad gleam in his eye.

"Oh dear, he must have broken out of the greenhouse!" said Mom. "I'd better see if I can help."

She started running after the fast disappearing procession shouting, "Mr. Willoughby, come back. You mustn't overdo it, you know. Come and have a nice soothing cup of herbal tea..."

I sighed and went back into the house.

It had definitely been one of those days.

And it wasn't over yet!

Chapter Five

The Secret Enemy

It looked as if lunch was going to be a do-it-yourself affair, so I went back in the kitchen and got myself a glass of milk and a cheese sandwich.

For once the house was quiet. Gran and Grandpa had gone off to their respective attic and basement, in disgrace. Dad had gone back to his study, Meg had disappeared to her room, and Murdo *still* wasn't up.

When I'd finished my lunch I went up to my room and stretched out on the bed. I wasn't dozing though—I was thinking hard.

It seemed to me that everyone was so concerned with what had been happening that no one was giving any thought to *why* it had happened.

I thought back to the beginning of it all, to that weird business at the mall. There was that strange magic mist... Then I'd had a few idle thoughts about jungles and gorillas and it had all gotten out of hand.

That reminded me of what Grandpa had said. His feud with Gran had gotten out of hand also. And so had Mom's medicines, producing a far too energetic Mr. Willoughby.

Then there was Meg and the strange way she'd been acting. Somehow there seemed to be a sort of pattern.

I stared up at the shelf over the end of my bed. Instead of Old Ted, there was the new Ted, the bear Meg had bought for me—and suddenly I knew I had to talk to Meg.

Taking the bear from the shelf, I went along the hall to her room. I tapped on the door.

A muffled voice called, "Yes?"

"It's me, Mike," I said, and went inside.

I hadn't been in Meg's room for quite a while, but it hadn't changed. Still amazingly

neat and tidy, not like mine which was a total mess. Everything in quiet, peaceful colors—except for the flashy movie and theater posters on the walls.

Meg was stretched out on her bed, lying face down, her head buried in a pillow.

She twisted her head around as I came in. "What is it? What do you want?"

"I need to talk to you."

"Can't it wait? I'm not feeling too well."

"I'm not feeling all that wonderful myself," I snapped. "But we've still got to talk."

It wasn't the way I usually spoke to Meg, and she looked surprised, and a bit alarmed.

She wriggled around on the bed and sat up. "Go on then—talk!"

When it actually came to the point, it was hard to begin. "Well, it's just that, recently, you seem to have been a bit strange, not really like yourself..." I mumbled. "Come on, Meg, you know we are the only sensible people in this family. I mean, we always used to get along so well but recently..."

"Oh don't start all that again, Mike," she said wearily. "I told you, you're imagining things."

I shook my head. "You were going to tell me something, earlier, in the kitchen, when the family turned up. Why don't you tell me now? Maybe I can help."

Meg's hair was hanging loose, and she started pushing it back in its usual severe-looking bun. "I'm sorry, Mike, maybe I have been a bit out of sorts—but can you wonder? I mean, with all these upsets."

I shook my head. "I'm talking about before the trouble—though I do think there's a connection."

"What do you mean, a connection?'

"Between you, and the trouble—and Angus."

She jumped up in a rage. "How dare you say that? You've got no reason at all..."

I held up the new teddy bear. "Oh yes, I have, Meg. This!"

Suddenly Meg blew up. "Can't I have a life of my own without you poking and prying all the time?" She snatched the teddy bear and hurled it across the room. "If you don't want the teddy bear you can throw it away!"

She grabbed a coat and stormed out of the room. A moment later I heard the front door slam behind her.

I waited a few moments and slipped out

after her. I saw her hurrying down the street and followed at a safe distance, making sure she didn't see me. It didn't surprise me in the least when she headed straight for the mall again.

She went to the door of the AM Games shop and Angus came out to greet her. He was still tall and dark but he didn't look quite so handsome—not with several bandages on his cheek.

All my worst fears were confirmed.

The kiss was a lot shorter this time. Meg pulled away frowning and they went inside.

I waited for a minute or two and then went to look for the mall's store directory.

A few minutes later, I followed Meg into the shop.

She was at the back in a huddle with Angus. They were standing close together, and they leaped guiltily apart when I appeared. "Mike, really!" said Meg angrily. "What did I just say to you? Do you have to follow me everywhere? Haven't you ever heard of tact?"

"I think we've gotten a bit beyond tact," I said sadly. "Tell me something, Angus, what does the M in AM stand for?"

"Mactavish—Angus Mactavish."

I shook my head. "I don't think so. It's written on the store directory as plain as anything. 'AM Games—proprietor Angus MacAroon'."

Meg's new boyfriend came from the clan of our oldest enemy.

"All right, so you know then," said Meg defiantly. "Angus and I love each other, and we don't care about this ridiculous feud."

"Are you sure?" I asked. "I think Angus must care a great deal."

Angus didn't speak and immediately Meg flared up in his defense. "What do you mean by that?"

"What do *you* mean Meg, taking things from our house to give him? Dad's slipper, Mom's cookbook, Grandpa's smoking jacket, my old teddy bear. The new teddy bear gave the game away. You bought me a replacement before I even told you Old Teddy was missing. There was only one way you could have known."

Meg looked guilty, but she was still defiant. "Angus needed those things for his studies. He's not fully qualified yet, and he wanted to study them, to learn from our magic power."

I shook my head. "Come off it, Meg. All those things were old and treasured—they held some of our spiritual power. Angus studied them all right, and he used them to ruin our magic, to boost it to make trouble for us." I looked accusingly at Angus. "You caused that gorilla illusion in the mall—and you called if off when Meg got involved. I

think you're behind our other problems too. Mom's medicine going into overdrive, Gran and Grandpa staging a public dogfight... anything to make the people of the town suspicious and afraid. I think there's more to come. We'll be lucky if we're not driven out of town, or torn to pieces by an angry mob."

"It's not true," Meg pleaded. "It's not true—is it, Angus?"

"It's true," I said. "Or else why did he kidnap Grimalkin, the one thing sure to set Gran on the rampage? That would have been too much even for you to swallow. He had to do that himself. Only, Grimalkin escaped, and left his mark behind him."

I pointed to the bandages on Angus's face.

Meg looked at Angus and he bowed his head. "It's all true, Meg, everything the laddie says. I was sent here by my grandfather, The MacAroon of MacAroon to make trouble for your family—and to stop your father from becoming President of the Institute of Practitioners in Magic."

Witches can't cry, but I could have sworn there were tears in Meg's eyes. "But you said you loved me..."

"And that's true as well," said Angus. "But by the time I realized I really loved you, I'd gone too far to draw back. Can you ever forgive me?"

"No," said Meg. "I can't. I never want to see you again."

She turned and marched out of the shop.

I waited and turned to Angus. "I think you've still got some of our property."

He took a box from under the counter. It held Dad's other slipper, Mom's cookbook, Grandpa's smoking jacket, Murdo's cloak and my battered Old Teddy.

I took the box. "If you really loved Meg you'd help to make things right again."

"It's too late now," said Angus gloomily. "The spell for the Mist of Malice was given to me by my grandfather. I canna undo it even if I wanted to."

"Thanks a lot," I said. Picking up the box, I followed Meg from the shop.

I found her in the mall, just standing there, staring into space. "I knew something was going on, Mike," she said. "I just didn't want to face it. Can you understand that?"

I gave her an awkward pat on the shoulder.

"Come on, Meg," I said. "Let's go home."

I called a family meeting when I got back. I felt sorry for Meg, but it was the only thing to do.

Meg just sat there staring into space while I told the whole story—including the bit about the gorilla in the mall.

For once Dad didn't yell at me or tell me off. He didn't say anything to Meg either, but I don't think it made her feel any better.

When I'd finished she said, "I'm sorry, everyone. This is all my fault. I can't believe how I fell for all that nonsense he told me. It's as if I was under a spell—and I'm not used to that. That was what was so wonderful about meeting Angus. I knew he was immune to the Glamor, so I thought he must really love me."

Mom leaned forward and patted Meg's hand. "I think you *were* under a spell, dear," she said. "The oldest one of all. It's called falling in love, and even MacMagics aren't immune."

Impatient with all this sentiment, Dad cleared his throat. "Listen carefully, all of you! My enemy the MacAroon of MacAroon has summoned up the Mist of Malice. It's a very powerful spell, and one that's very hard to get rid of. It will hang around us for some time yet—and it means that any time we use the Power, the effects will be unpredictable and dangerous—as we have all seen."

Practical as ever, Mom said, "Well, it's all very unfortunate, but if it's happened, it's happened. What are we going to do about it?"

"Naturally we shall counteract the spell," said Dad huffily. "But it will be difficult and

dangerous, and it will take time, twenty-four hours at least. Meanwhile we must all stay at home—and no one is to use any magic whatsoever, until I give the word that it's safe. Do you all understand?"

We all nodded in agreement, and the meeting broke up.

Mom and Dad and Gran and Grandpa went off to work on the counterspells, Meg went to lie down, and I went off to my room. It's harder than you might think to sit still and do nothing, and out of sheer boredom I decided to get on with my homework. I worked steadily for several hours and by the time I got it all done it was getting dark.

I noticed the cardboard box on the end of my bed and took out Old Ted, sitting him on the shelf with his new companion. I'd already given Dad his missing slipper, Grandpa his smoking jacket and Mom her cookbook, but there was still something black folded at the bottom of the box. I took it out and unfolded it. It was Murdo's old vampire cloak. It was only then I realized—we'd forgotten Murdo.

It was quite understandable. Old Murdo's such a useless wimp that it's easy to overlook him. Anyway, there was no harm done. I'd just go down, wake him up and warn him to stay at home tonight.

With the cloak over my arm I went down to his basement bedroom. The door was open and the coffin-bed with its black silk sheets was empty. Murdo's other cloak, his new one, was gone from the peg behind the door.

Murdo the would-be vampire was out on the town.

Outside, in the dark, the Mist of Malice was waiting…

Chapter Six

Out for Blood

Murdo had to be found and brought back right away, and with my parents and grandparents busy and Meg still feeling awful, it was up to me.

At least I knew where to start looking. Murdo's favorite spot in town is the graveyard around the church. It's dark and creepy and overgrown, just the place for a would-be vampire.

Jane the minister's daughter was Murdo's girlfriend and they used to meet there in the evenings. Jane was away on vacation at the moment, but Murdo was still fond of hanging around there like a lost soul.

Anyway, it was somewhere to start.

I visualized the old graveyard and zapped myself right to the spot.

Despite being near the middle of town the old walled graveyard was dark and spooky. The paving stones of the winding paths were covered with moss, the walls dripped with ivy, and around the massive dark bulk of the church, the tombstones leaned at crazy angles.

A faint mist hung in the air and I shuddered, fearing the worst. The air felt damp and chilly and I'd come outside without a coat. I was still carrying Murdo's cloak though, and I wrapped it around me for warmth. Murdo was nowhere to be seen.

"Murdo!" I hissed. "Murdo, where are you?"

There was no reply.

Suddenly I heard the tapping of high-heeled shoes on the flagstones. The church and the graveyard are set between the old main street and the new shopping area and people often used the churchyard as a shortcut.

A girl was doing it now, coming from the main street to the shopping area. She was wearing a white raincoat, and the light of the churchyard lamp gleamed on her fair hair.

I didn't want to frighten her, so I ducked down out of sight behind the nearest tombstone.

Obviously a bit nervous, the girl hurried along the path. There was a mausoleum at the far end, a sort of square stone hut. Just as she reached it, Murdo leaped out from behind it.

He was dressed up in the full vampire gear, black clothes, long black cloak, white face and gleaming red eyes.

Not surprisingly, he gave the poor girl a nasty shock and she jumped back with a little scream.

Then she smiled. "Oh it's you, Murdo. Didn't you know, Jane's on vacation?"

Murdo just glared wildly at her and snarled.

The girl looked puzzled. "You remember me, Jane's friend Emma? We met at the church tea party?"

Murdo gave a blood-curdling growl and leaped on her, trying to sink his teeth in her neck.

The Mist of Malice was at work and poor Murdo was possessed. I ran to help—help the girl I mean—but I really needn't have bothered.

However much they may seem to like this sort of thing in movies, young ladies don't care for it in real life.

Emma was a big strong girl and Murdo, possessed or not, was still pretty much a weakling. She struggled and lashed out wildly, trying to beat off her attacker.

Even as a child, Murdo had a sensitive nose. He was always having nosebleeds and even now the slightest tap would set him off. One of Emily's waving fists landed smack on his nose and a fountain of blood jetted out.

I'd come up to them by now and I heaved Murdo away.

"It's all right, he won't hurt you," I said.

Never try to reassure a nervous girl in a

lonely churchyard when you're wrapped up in a vampire cloak.

She gave a piercing scream, gave me a clip around the ear that made my head spin, and dashed out into the crowded shopping center. A great splash of blood—Murdo's blood—stained the front of her white coat. She looked like something out of a horror movie and not surprisingly a crowd gathered around her right away.

I watched from the shadows by the churchyard gate.

The mist drifted from the churchyard and hung around the little crowd.

In the front of the crowd was a gang of men out for a night on the town. By the sound of them, they'd had quite a few beers already.

"Who did it, honey?" one of them asked. "Who attacked you?"

"Murdo MacMagic..." gasped Emma. "In the churchyard. His brother was with him." The mist swirled thicker, and her voice rose hysterically. "They're vampires, both of them."

An angry murmur ran through the little

crowd. "MacMagics... it's the MacMagics..."

"Always causing trouble, those MacMagics," someone shouted. "Look at that business in the mall this morning—and in town this afternoon! We should get rid of them, run them out of town." A roar of assent went up. The evil mist was working on the crowd as well.

"We know where they live!" shouted someone else. "We'll go up there and drive them out!"

"Let's deal with these vampires first," shouted one of the men who was standing just outside a hardware shop.

"We all know what happens to vampires! We can get what we need in here."

The other men helped to kick in the window as they all disappeared inside the shop.

Seconds later they were out again, clutching hammers and mallets and what looked like some kind of fencing stakes. With a shudder I noticed that the stakes were already sharpened at one end.

I shot back into the churchyard where Murdo was trying to stop the flow of blood from his nose with a grubby handkerchief.

I was relieved to see that the mad gleam had gone from his eyes.

"I can't think what got into me," he gasped. "You know I wouldn't hurt anyone, Mike. I'm not a real vampire."

I heard angry shouts and the sound of running feet.

"A stake through the heart will kill you

really dead though," I said. "Come on, Murdo, we've got to get away from here."

Teleporting yourself is pretty basic, but like all magic it needs concentration. Murdo was too shaken up to think straight.

"Concentrate, Murdo," I urged. "Think of home—and get yourself back there, right now!"

Murdo just stared blankly at me—and the leaders of the stake and hammer mob rushed into the churchyard.

"Do it, Murdo," I shouted. "Now!"

The sight of all those sharpened stakes jolted old Murdo out of his trance. He drew a deep breath—and vanished with a faint pop, as the air filled the vacuum where he'd been.

The crowd fell back for a moment, with a gasp of awe. "It's the work of the devil!" one of them shouted.

Someone a bit braver yelled, "Grab the other one before he gets away."

The crowd surged forward.

We were breaking all the rules using magic in front of everyone but there didn't seem to be any alternative.

As the leader grabbed the edge of my cloak I vanished too, leaving the empty cloak in his grasp.

Back home I called a family meeting and told them the bad news. Dad looked really worried. "The Mist of Malice boosts and distorts people's emotions. That's why that crowd got so excited so quickly. I'm afraid it's all too likely they'll come up here and attack us."

Grandpa said, "We can still manage to frighten them off, surely. A few harmless bangs and flashes and they'll run away."

"We can try," said Dad. "But with the Mist still in operation—well, it might not work."

"It might work all too well," said Mom quietly. "Suppose we end up really hurting people, perhaps even killing them. Whatever happened, we'd never live it down."

"This is all my fault," said Meg. "If I hadn't fallen for Angus…"

Murdo didn't say anything; he was still sniveling into his handkerchief.

I looked out of the window and saw a group of flaring lights at the end of the road.

"Whatever we're doing, we'd better get on with it," I said. "The traditional mob with blazing torches is coming up the street."

"We'll go out and face them together," said Dad. "If we combine our Powers, we may still be able to drive them off without hurting them."

We went out of our front door to face the mob.

They were there outside our front gate, and already they were shrouded in mist.

An angry roar went up as we appeared,

like the voice of one huge animal.

"There they are!" shouted one of the leaders. "Burn them! Burn them out!"

He started up the driveway brandishing his torch.

Grandpa snapped his fingers and a fireball exploded at the man's feet.

The man jumped back with a yell. Then, when he realized he wasn't hurt he came forward again, and the crowd started to follow. It was going to take more than a few magic fireworks to scare this group off.

I looked up at Dad's tense face. I knew he and Grandpa between them could call down a firestorm that would fry most of the crowd to a crisp—and start a witch-hunt that would sweep the whole country.

We were in a no-win situation, blamed if we fought back and doomed if we didn't.

A weird wailing sound filled the air.

It was coming from the other side of the house and everyone turned to look.

A tall kilted figure appeared, stalking toward us and playing the bagpipes.

"It's Angus!" gasped Meg.

"He's picked a funny time to come and

serenade you!"

"Hush, laddie," said Grandpa. "That's no ordinary tune. Look!"

There was a black cloud over Angus's head, and it seemed to be following him.

Then it drifted forward until it hung over the astonished crowd.

As the pipes wailed on, the black cloud was suddenly split by a jagged streak of lightning.

There was an ear-splitting clap of thunder

and it started to rain as if someone had turned on a giant tap.

The torrential rain poured down on the little crowd, putting out their torches. They made no attempt to escape. They just stood there, staring upward as the rain beat down into their faces, soaking them to the skin, and washing away the evil mist.

The sound of the pipes changed key and the cloud and the rainstorm drifted away toward the town.

The crowd moved off after it.

The leader, the man who'd been all set to burn our house down, turned to Dad with a friendly grin. "Wet night, Mr. MacMagic! Still, good for the gardens, eh?"

He moved away from the others.

"He'll remember nothing of what's happened by tomorrow," said Grandpa. "Nor will the others, or anyone else in town. Everything's back to normal." He turned to Angus as the sound of the pipes died away. "The Lament of Forgetting and the Rains of Oblivion. That was it, wasn't it, laddie? I haven't seen that old spell used in years."

Angus looked appealingly at Meg. "I just

had to do something to make things right, and I remembered this ancient spell…it took me ages to get it just right."

Meg rushed up to him and hugged him. "You look so handsome in the kilt," she said and kissed him.

Angus blushed.

"Well done, young man," said Dad. "Whatever harm you did us, you certainly

have succeeded in making amends."

"My grandfather the MacAroon will no' be so pleased," said Angus gloomily. "He promised to make me a full magician if I made his plan work. I'll be in for it now..."

"The old villain won't harm you," said Dad confidently. "Not unless he wants this whole disgraceful tale made public. You're talking to the next President of the Institute of Practitioners in Magic, remember. I'll make you a full magician myself at the Conference. That was as fine a piece of natural weather magic as I've ever seen."

"Yes, and we're very grateful," said Mom. "You must come in for a cup of coffee."

Dad took Angus by the arm. "I think we'd

better have a little chat, young man. Now what, precisely, are your intentions toward my daughter?"

Dad and Angus, Meg and Mom, Gran and Grandpa all went back inside the house.

I turned to Murdo whose nose had stopped bleeding at last. "Sunday tomorrow, Murdo! Nothing ever happens on a Sunday. We can have a nice rest."

I kept my fingers crossed though.

You never know what's going to happen next—when you're a MacMagic!

More Exciting Adventures With Arch Books

Arch Books are Barron's gripping mini-novels for children of various reading ages. Each of the titles in this series offers the young reader a special adventure. The stories are packed with action, humor, mystery, chilling thrills and even a bit of magic! Each paperback book boasts 12 to 24 handsome line-art illustrations. Each book: $2.95, Can. $3.95 (those marked with an * are $3.50, Can. $4.25.) (Ages 6–11)

Arch Book Titles:

BEN AND THE CHILD OF THE FOREST
ISBN: 3936-X

THE BLUEBEARDS: Adventure on Skull Island
ISBN: 4421-5

THE BLUEBEARDS: Mystery at Musket Bay
ISBN: 4422-3

THE BLUEBEARDS: Peril at the Pirate School
ISBN: 4502-5

THE BLUEBEARDS: Revenge at Ryan's Reef*
ISBN: 4903-9

CAROLINE MOVES IN
ISBN: 3938-6

A CAT CALLED MAX: Magnificent Max
ISBN: 4427-4

A CAT CALLED MAX: Max and the Quiz Kids
ISBN: 4501-7

A CAT CALLED MAX: Max's Amazing Summer*
ISBN: 4819-9

IN CONTROL, MS. WIZ?
ISBN: 4500-9

INTO THE NIGHT HOUSE
ISBN: 4423-1

MEET THE MACMAGICS*
ISBN: 4882-2

MS. WIZ SPELLS TROUBLE
ISBN: 4420-7

THE MACMAGICS: A Spell for My Sister*
ISBN: 4881-4

THE MACMAGICS: My Brother the Vampire*
ISBN: 4883-0

THE RED SPORTS CAR
ISBN: 3937-8

YOU'RE UNDER ARREST, MS. WIZ
ISBN: 4499-1

All prices are in U.S. and Canadian dollars and subject to change without notice. At your bookstore or order direct adding 10% postage (minimum charge $1.75—Canada $2.00). N.Y. residents add sales tax.
ISBN PREFIX: 0-8120

Barron's Educational Series, Inc.
250 Wireless Blvd., Hauppauge, NY 11788
Call toll-free: 1-800-645-3476
In Canada: Georgetown Book Warehouse,
34 Armstrong Ave., Georgetown, Ont. L7G 4R9
Call toll-free: 1-800-247-7160